I0606655

RIVER ROCK
MOTORCYCLE GIRL

RIVER ROCK
MOTORCYCLE GIRL

J. Price

Cover photographed by Maxwell Hailstone

Copyright © 2020, J. Price

All rights reserved. Printed in the U.S.A.

No part of this publication may be reproduced or transmitted
in any form or by any means, electronic or mechanical,
including photocopy, recording or any information storage and
retrieval system now known or to be invented,
without permission in writing from the publisher,
except by a reviewer who wishes to quote brief passages
in connection with a review written for inclusion in a magazine,
newspaper or broadcast.

Quantity Purchases:
Companies, professional groups, clubs, and other
organizations may qualify for special terms when ordering
quantities of this title.
For information, email info@ebooks2go.net,
or call (847) 598-1150 ext. 4141.
www.ebooks2go.net

Published in the United States by eBooks2go, Inc. 1827 Walden
Office Square, Suite 260, Schaumburg, IL 60173

ISBN: 978-1-5457-5299-9

Library of Congress Cataloging in Publication

TABLE OF CONTENTS

LIST OF ILLUSTRATIONS

CHAPTER 1

INNOCENCE

The Preparation for this journey began long before the first days of awareness. Golden sun sinks into pink foam, lilacs bloom purple with yellow dandelions, awakening the green grass memories of running across the Thunderbird Indian Mound's wings; waiting, wanting to climb the high rocks, up to the eagles' sky, to speak with the ancient ones. Voices cry out from the past, don't you remember little one?

Waiting, wanting, the beginnings of desire, encompassing an entire realm of physical, spiritual aspects, all leaning toward the great discovery. Fueling all activity, the goal of the moment, Ellie watched her first unearthing, the orange bull dozer pushed a Conical Indian Mound into Lake Wakanda in 1961. Underneath the dome, the musty black earth was entangled among jumbled bones and a feathered headdress. Blackened leather evidenced the clumsy bulldozing, its pieces surrounded the scooped up confusion. This one was not so ancient, such a massive grave robbery by the Historical Society, perhaps they needed a new headdress for their display.

Her heart pounded as she peered into the pitted tomb, a mass of arrowheads, copper pipes and Indian beads. Call the Winnebago, Grandpa's been dug up! Why stand at the edge to look into both death and resurrection? She ran excitedly to the front yard where the green striped snakes surrounded the site, watching as they slithered towards the cement pond for decapitation by her older brother. What a strangely, joyous mood surrounded this awkward exhuming. At the age of six, she had witnessed the removal of a family of skeletons, still clothed in their deer skins and feathers. They were off to the Museum, where they belong, said the state archeologists, and all will be well.

A decade later, on the other side of the railroad tracks, where the bikes go, she discovered something very early on, the addiction of Harley thunder. Ellie was the feminine tomboy at the age of sixteen. Her long blonde hair curled about her shoulders, framing a rather determined face. Years of ballet graced her form, one that would evolve into muscular defiance. Janis Joplin was her hero because she would not take any lip, 'cause nobody could tell her what to do and she thrived on being the boss. She did not recognize her own femininity or blue-eyed blonde looks, only a stubborn instance upon her rebellious stormy independence, a most difficult, fiery child had emerged into the defiant one.

Right now she was running up the cement slab steps, to discover the Clubhouse. She had heard so much talk about the place and was bold enough to enter. They say once you have had a taste, you'll always return. She stormed across the splintered wood floor, there at the end of the bar was the Rotted President, Misty Dee on his lap, nearly covered in black leather. His face shone as an angel's radiating pink velvet ribbons of light. Who wonders what they do in there? At 16, an eye full of kisses would tend to evoke jealousy, but no, only the determination, the willing of her soul to be there ten minutes earlier. Misty Dee tossed back her raven black hair, and wiping her lips with the back of her hand, she glared at Ellie for the first time, a thirty year glance, then spun around and toppled to the floor.

Rotted President said "Who is this intruder, how old is that girl, she shouldn't be in here!" Feeling stripped naked as the Rotted President angrily glanced at her, his eyes turned from rage to curiosity in a moment. Ellie just ignored him, stood firm at the end of the long wooden bar and ordered a Pepsi to go. She quickly glanced back at the Black Leather King and she felt her heart pound, then jump. Oh yah, here's one to remember. No matter, it was only daylight, but the longing to wear colors was born at that moment. Yet it was at second glance back that was solidified in her memory, far beyond his lifetime. A closer look revealed the small, handmade tattoos on his hands, LOVE on the right, HATE on the left, a small cross on the thumb's web and "Sally" somewhere in it all. Images that Ellie would remember long after his death, as they too were later pounded into her head, with extraordinary intensity. The very thought of Rotted blasted the Clubhouse order; long dark hair, beard and eyes that shot through your soul, he knew your every thought before you spoke. His intricate personality combined great intellect with commanding performance; he was always one step ahead of the ride.

In recognition, Ellie moved into the early evening, stepping past the black and chrome bikes, nearly gliding into the deep purple night sky. The day before she had spent an afternoon retreat in Panther Mound Park, where she watched the crimson sun sink into the calm summer lake. There was a 50 foot Indian Mound, nearly 5 feet tall and shaped like a bear, but because it had a short tail and was near the lake, it was labeled a Panther Mound. Ellie read about it long after she had played on top of it.

This particular Panther Mound had been excavated in 1945. A tunnel was discovered from the left paw extending to a central chamber located under the panther's chest. This architectural assemblage recalled Egypt's great sphinx. The tunnel led to a hollow room with compacted dirt walls and rotted timber. The chamber's center contained a truncated stone altar that was painted in red ochre. Deer bones, copper tools and stone pipes were scattered at the base. Ellie knew long ago the Panther Mound was hollow and would echo if you ran, jumped, stomped or drummed on it. The Indian Mounds had become her playgrounds. They decorated the landscape in numerous animal and geometric shapes.

However, the tomboy blonde had already settled on too many compromises to go back to the childhood thumping games. At the moment, Ellie was too concerned about guys to play those earth drumming games, besides who can run in high heels? The '60s child radiated an aura of patchouli, myrrh and Balsam of Peru, a combination that the guys preferred. Her spiked high heels with tiny black straps and silver buckles clashed with her jeans, hot pink polish and tight red top. Her angelic face would not reveal the true past history. Ellie always kept her secrets.

But now, due to a combination of events, Ellie's journey had just began, a one trip addiction to freedom, to pursue her own spiritual rebellion, which became an infinite quest. Forget the guys, she could do all things on her own, with no instructions. The Clubhouse was the new playground and had already cast its eternal holding spell upon her.

So later that evening, she crossed the railroad tracks, against the solstice wind, pressing forward to see the gleaming black bikes. The silver chrome thunderers echoed through the night. They stacked up outside the Clubhouse. Purple spikes toppled onto 16" rakes. Chrome forks were chopped way to far over; chain driven steel wrapped on cogs, long before the belts. The sleds were tossed along the pavement, concrete sidewalk and caliche outside the Clubhouse.

One hundred and fifty leather bad boys bent for the Friday night ride, beer drinking, busting, kicking or laying ass. She went back down to the Clubhouse, ran up those crooked, cracked steps to soak in the guys. Suddenly, just before the club ride, the most gorgeous Road Captain, Rider, bolted into the bar. Little Ellie could not figure out why God made guys made like this. He was not the first, but definitely one of the finest JDs, she had ever seen. A true Scorpio with brown wavy hair, a capricious grin and slender yet a muscularly defiant build, he had more strength than the ethereal Strider.

Once again, perhaps for the millionth time, her mind raced back to Strider, the only reason she rode, breathed, escaped, waited; someone she had continuously longed to see. The Clubhouse noise faded as her memory surged forward to catch a glimpse of Strider. The fleeting trance had grabbed her once again, a power rush of soft kisses, from a mischievous boy who was only getting to you for a few minutes. It was always just for a quick moment that he gave you everything, too fast to ever grasp.

Ellie had met Strider at Panther Mound Park, on the north shore of Lake Wakanda, on the flat top Pyramid Mound just before the May Day ride. All the Saturnians had ridden up from Beeville for the party. Over 40 black, purple and chrome sleds glided into position far beyond the parking lot. Scattered among the ancient ruins, in no particular order, each sled rang out its own presence with green, yellow or purple skulls, orange snakes, iron crosses or naked ladies.

Intricate chrome glistened in the sun, electric chrome handle bars, decorated valve covers, tapered cylinders, diced rims, dove tail bitch bars, or no back seat at all. A true biker, as the Road Queen would eventually realize, lives and rides alone.

Sitting tossed among the Serpent, Conical and Pyramidal Mounds, were two masses of blue-eyed blonde Norwegian muscle, whispering red wine girl secrets, two of the finest golden gods that Ellie had ever seen. Strider was sitting next to Bear Man. Her heart stopped beating, almost a complete stand still, while a melted brain lock of awareness, rivers of green, gold syrup, swam across her mind. The lock carried purple velvet ships with billowing marshmallow sails that ballooned into a momentarily softened crimson sky. The vision remained until he spoke, then the future was thrown in front of her, blasting forward three decades in one explosive expression. "Hey." He was a farm boy, he had tractor hands that moved ten times faster than anything she had ever seen or felt, after all, he ran 600 acres and 300 dairy... funny that he never mentioned his hired crew, because actually the dazzling shy charmer was spoiled rotten.

Her words tried to bubble out, not in English, but in Elvin tongue. Ah oh, she couldn't speak, she just stared at her new emergence. These were the days before salvation, when a primordial, primitive response drove one to insanity. How far would you go for that first kiss? Staring equally into tomorrow, next Saturday; the May Day Festival was marked on both calendars, sealed a sea of turquoise blue diamond eyes that shone into tomorrow. Finally she had found him, the one to dream endlessly upon, chase forever, to the jagged edge.

May Day Festival followed, filled with dead heads in multi-colored tie dyes, contrasting the orange and black HD T shirts, worn by east side muscle boys. They all gathered in front of a sound stage, adjacent to the jumping, glimmering bluegills, in ancient Winona Bay. Strider was alone, smiling. Looking so happy, he beamed when the conversation began. Strider was so fast, so nonverbal, blunt, too the point and rarely weakened to show his emotions. This youth had learned to harden all feelings by necessity; the girl he loved had been blown to pieces by a truck crossing Highway 100, while following him into a club. His heart hardened by guilt, an unnecessary burden which he would carry until his death, it had formed his personality.

It was tossed in your face; he let you know you'd never get close to him and his grief. His 14 year old baby doll was dead because of his ignorance or arrogance, something he'd never acknowledge. After all, all the girls ran after Strider.

Excepting that one afternoon, when a shy biker boy was embarrassingly loosing it, gleaming radiant joy, ribbons of happiness, anticipation flowed from his body. Tan, tall solid, only an occasional boyish grin would leave a tell tale sign. Ellie didn't care what anybody would ever say, Strider was in love over his head at first sight. Finally, he spoke.

"Ellie is it true that you're a bike mechanic and know the Rittman boys? I've heard some pretty amazing things about you." Strider began an inquisition. The problem was that Ellie was too blown away to verify. "Yah, yah." she mumbled, but blushed to look at him. Eyes large and wide, like saucers, she put her tiny, slender hand in his. There was always something awkward about Strider. He was gawky in his youth, as if he sprouted up too fast and had hit great sorrow too young. Ellie couldn't take her eyes off of him; it was an electric-chemical reaction with magneto energy.

Yah, she knew the Rittman boys, they had gotten her into all kinds of trouble, but that legend would be told later on. She glanced down at her bell bottoms with all nine multi-colored planets, stars and constellations carefully sown on them, including Orion and the Pleiades. He noticed them, but had merely smiled. No comment on the artistic ballerina side of this blonde, just the next blunt command.

"Let's go to the Cinnamon House now." he commanded. Ellie's reputation had preceded her, he must have heard about the Cinnamon House from the Rittman boys. Her mind raced to her place, an old farm house, miles away where other stories emerged. The Cinnamon House was an equilateral legend. It was a universal oscillating point between time and space, with a 200 acre apple orchard. A place where the smell of fresh baked cinnamon apple pie and zucchini bread lingered for hours, it had a magic garden with spring fed asparagus, entangled with pumpkin vines, broccoli, tomatoes and sweet peas.

Yet strange things happened at the Cinnamon House farm. It once contained an 1870 red schoolhouse which still echoed with the children's voices. Ellie recalled climbing an apple tree, hearing soft giggles behind her, right before she slipped several feet down, when her sweat pants' cord had caught the branch. She hung there, suspended in the apple tree, above the ground for hours, a great ghost given wedgy.

But Strider was now questioning her, what to do, what to do, yes, she wanted him, but it was always her place, on his terms and right at the moment. OK, OK. A deep pit murmuring of sin transcribed her stomach, a little kicker that was an addicting rush. But did she really feel that this early May Day, or was that later instilled in her memory after obtaining multi-colored wings? Try to remember that precise moment between innocent love and corrupted desire. Honestly, at the May Day Festival that spring, she was head over heels in love with what she thought was IT, the number one dude in the whole world. Therefore, whatever he wanted or she wanted was 100 percent fine in God's universe. It didn't matter as being in love excludes all conditions, or so Ellie believed at the time. So, she murmured "Let's go." They rode out on his black and chrome 1969 Sportster and after the 20 mile shake up, the rest was a blur.

Sunset's golden glow filled the white room, pink and red crystal glass reflections danced on the carpet, entangled in a single bed, their vision merged for a life time. Ellie would always see Strider's dreams. Purple cubed cut glass with streams of green, like a waterfall running down one's back, leading the viewer to the next scenario. Turquoise brilliant blue diamond eyes sparkled with true joy; they matched the deep orange coral kisses. Their paths crossed for years, leaving town to meet him, while he's going to your place, missing each other over, over and over; they were star-crossed lovers.

CHAPTER 2

INITIATION

It was without reservation that Ellie drove her '65 Mustang down to Beeville, chasing that farm boy, wearing 6" platform shoes, tight size 3 jeans, a white laced bodice, with sea shell buttons tied with a pink ribbon. Three weeks had passed with no word from Strider, which provided the fuel for her Valley quest.

Pounding down rum and cokes to hide her pounding heart, it took every ounce of nerve to make the 60 mile journey into the Ancient Valley. The Saturnarians had a hold over the Ancient Valley, they ruled from a distance, and now she was in the center of their domain, Louie's Bar.

Talking and talking, she stared into tomorrow, on an ocean of crystal blue eyes, blushing again into shy wonder, thinking about those bikes, waiting for a second chance kiss. Louie's Bar centered around a curved oak bar rail that held a specific collection of old drooling drunks, Marlboro farm boys, leather boy bikers and the bossiest chicks Ellie had ever seen. Boy, why did she think she would ever blend in? It was the days of a rebellious John Deere hog town without country western, just acid rock and roll, the Doors, Stones and much later on AC/DC.

Buck up, she thought, who else had learned to ride on that little Honda, crossing over the cliffs down at Winona Bay Park. She could jump over anything, pull wheelies and rip apart that sled faster than most. Then why should she be so disarmed, so intimated by these guys? Besides it was lame tame compared to the Clubhouse, after all, everyone had their clothes on.

Ellie thought back to just a few years earlier, when she was on the back of that dirt bike going over a stony path, racing up hill doing jumps, leaps and spin outs. Her legs were wrapped so tightly around this other guy, who was and still is, untamable. It was the totally wild, and the "you can't have me" attitude that she always fell for. Actually, in hind sight, it was a mix of the leg wrapping, the roaring engine and attitude which appealed to Ellie.

This other younger, wild one was Strider's childhood friend, someone that had hurt her so bad, she couldn't remember his name. He was so very impenetrable, aloof, driftless and yet he was the one who taught her how to shift gears and leave go. Her mind could still recall his pleading words "Ellie, ya gotta learn to leave go, let go of me, 'cause I gotta be free." He begged her to be free and so he was.

However, perhaps this was the initiation for one of her life's themes. Ellie would never be nobody's nothing, or so she thought at the time; she'd never belong to anyone. Not because she had already loved too deeply, but because her spirit had to shake off all chains, all clamp downs on her every action, word and deed. She was the Road Queen, for a number of reasons. At a great expense to Ellie, but it was worth it, as it became a method for riding and living; one down, four up and let it rip.

Then bang, it was back to the bikes, the gleaming steel machines began to spit fire and smoke, as they fired up outside of Louie's Bar. Ellie ran to catch up, to be a part of this action, but no, the great abandonment began to happen, the reality of being left alone on the sidewalk, the predictable, yet very painful, dump. She watched the 20 bikes roll out, their thunder shakes the windows. Legs aching, now waiting for Strider, her heart sinking, the sorrow overwhelming, but no one would know it.

Now the bikers are gone, rolled away into bliss and its dark, only 10 p.m. on a Saturday night.

So she glided back into Louie's Bar, the clock slows down as the locals stumble in, too late to drive back... tick tock... too far to go home, she was hopeless. Slamming down the drinks, switching from rum cokes to 151 shots, the longing for him grew. More people come in to stare, Ellie wondered how many times they had played this scene out, how many stray kittens were absolved, tossed back into the night.

Midnight comes around, a messenger appears, a sole Saturnian enters, but ignores, just totally ignores her. Ellie decides to break all the rules by gathering information as quickly as possible and find that party place. No, she hadn't been sent for, she was on her own, risking it all by asking directions. Go up County T, to the left, third caliche road will take her to that two story farm house. Racing to Mustang Sally, she accelerated to 125 m.p.h. flying down the blacktop, left, then right to the gravel road to the dilapidated, two story, white farm house.

The concrete steps were chipped and crooked and Ellie cringed as she entered the house. Now it appeared, unmistakably a deep gnawing in her stomach; 'cause she only wanted one thing from this dude. Fingers tingling as she opened the rough wooden door, four dudes in the first room, the aroma of incense, flowers on the table, but of no interest. But then, who lies collapsed in the corner, in a sea of euphoric bliss, just grinning while sprawled out on the floor, was the Free Strider.

Oh no, she muttered, how was she going to get him down? He was too high, they're always too high, she noted. It actually took a great deal of courage to barge into the Club's party and jump upon the passed out leader, and smother him in kisses. So Ellie just started kissing and kissing him 'till Strider finally said "Ah Jesus, just get upstairs, little girl." It took all of three minutes to get him up there. It was a mind blowing evening for that motorcycle girl who slipped into euphoria, releasing all elements, dying and living at the same time. God should not make guys like this, Strider was the best, ribbons of red velvet pushing up toward green, but then blue silver light ties the thread of eternity.

Crumpled, torn, ripped apart, Ellie could not move or speak, yet in that moment prior to the ultimate Road Queen abandonment, the price which would have to be paid for that May evening, when waiting to lie in the afterglow of his arms, but forget it that would never happen, he gets up and starts to put on his shoes. However, out of the silver blue, surprisingly out of nowhere, Strider speaks. "Oh Thunder Girl, do you know about the ancient caves? I have been in them!"

Shocked, Ellie stammered "No baby, tell me 'cause you know I am the one who runs across the Indian Mounds just to wonder why they echo, why the spirits dance on top of them under a full moon. Why those ancient spirits whisper to me, showing me the small white buffalo, raising his head in acknowledgement. He watches the Indian spirits dance above the mounds from the water.

The image appeared as she spoke to him, a reclining luminescent, white spirit bison with topaz eyes floated in the silver blue sky. He alights on top of the water, above the three foot rolling waves of Lake Wakanda, down at Waverly Park.

"Really, Strider, I've seen it! Blue waves cresting white foam under darkened stormy skies. The rhythmical pounding of these white and gray waves crush sea shells and pebbles and echo through time. The white bison lifts his head above the water floating in a blue-gray mist and he stares again towards me, as I listen to the waves now coating the pebbles in yellow, blue, gold and red, they glitter from the mouth of the lake shore cave." "You know," stammered Ellie, "the cave of golden sunshine trinkets from the before days."

"So tell me pretty baby boy, what do you see and where have you been, because you know that I'm the only one who will understand your mystic vision quest." Ellie waited in anticipation, waited for a vision, never expecting the information she was about to receive.

Stammering, stuttering as he glowed so pink, beaming in pure sex, Ellie thought "Why couldn't he understand I was his, why couldn't he see it? I was the only one who could make him smile so sweetly, she pondered, but no one ever gets Strider, the Free Strider.

He glanced down, Ellie thought, like my little brother, my lover, my best friend forever and rolled back his eyes. He lay back down on the bed. "Oh baby," she thought, "forget the story and please just hold me", but that couldn't happen until decades later, so right then, her soul screamed inside. Crisp linen, line-dried sheets, were permeated with peach kisses. A purple and blue lilac fragrance filled the room while curved spider webs danced in the breeze. Thirty years later she could still taste the kisses. What she didn't know, then, was another girl had dried the sheets.

Strider began slowly "Me and Mickey were six years old when we went down to Hilger's Farm, way down into the Valley by the creek bend.

We had heard the ghostly gold stories and wanted to look inside the Big Cave for ourselves. So we climbed halfway up the hill. The secret opening was under a flat rock, hidden in the hillside's indentation by some boulders. We dug under the rock and pushed it to the side and were small enough to go inside the tunnel. First on our backs, through the crevices, then scooting in sideways, twisting and turning through the small carved opening, clutching the rocks just enough just to shove through the tunnel to a small cavern entrance way. The first entrance room was filled with snakes and it smelled musty and echoed as if it were hollow.

Mickey had a flashlight and landed first, so we walked through the entrance chamber to a larger area. This room was very dark and full of serpents. The stone brown walls were coated with water and lichen. On the sides of the chamber were two stacked, stone slabs, like tables attached to a rock wall. On the slabs was a small or medium skeleton, each with copper crescent moon crown on their head. It appeared as if three small children and a mother were entombed here. The tall ceiling of this King's chamber looked like popcorn, composed of stone brown and white bubblegum drops.

In the middle of the big room was a large stone slab altar, raised about four feet off the ground. It contained a large skeleton, with a gold crescent moon crown. He was covered in sea shells and a gold shield was placed near his side. In the corner was a pile of shiny gray stones and arrowheads. Some of the stones had strange writing on them, like Egyptian hieroglyphics. Many more shiny shields were piled in the corner, along with large jars and swords.

Across the room, was an entrance to another chamber, where large copper statues towered in the dark cavern. Eight foot copper and stone figures, both bearded and robed, recalled Gothic Cathedral door jam saints. Some of the Elders looked down towards a large oval boulder in front of them, while others peered towards a third chamber that housed hundreds of carved stone tablets. White, blue and brown stalactites divided the room. In the far back corner, up a steep flight of stone steps was the third room, a library containing tombstone-shaped tablets carved with strange glyphs. Suddenly, the flashlight began to flicker, panic set in, the black snakes slithered too closely, and terror seized us.

We quickly ran out and squirmed our way up the tunnel to daylight." Strider said. "When asked by the farmer, "What did you see down there?" we were speechless, so the cave was dynamited shut and forever sealed.

"So, do you know this too, Ellie?" Strider asked. He sighed and looked up and commanded "I don't want you to talk about this ever again, do you understand?"

Ellie was dazed, she answered "Of course, I believe you Strider you're talking to the Road Queen of visions. I see underground of those Indian mounds and they talk to me. Those copper pipes resonate with musical notes. You know, the copper scepters held by the great chiefs that chime under piles of earth, but do you want to hear my story?"

But no time, he got up, nonverbal again and said "It's not my room you sleep here, I gotta go downstairs." Ellie passed out. Morning came and Ellie awoke with Strider hollering "Get up now, you gotta go, now!" He was standing at the bottom of the stairs.

Apparently Ellie had turned into poison during the night. He was keeping his distance. One of the most outstanding memories of her life was trying to get down those steep stairs, her legs buckled beneath her, thighs shaking, body aching; she was totally numb, tingling from head to toe.

He walked her out to her Mustang, at 6 a.m., said he had to do chores. Later she would find out it was just an excuse to get her out of there, as the regular girls would be home soon. Once again, Ellie had broken every rule, been where she should not have been, played the outsider at such a great price. She pleaded "No, don't go," something she would never do again, but he said go, so she was gone.

After all, the burn was on, the shocking deep pains of the wake up call. The pain of betrayal sunk deep into her soul, her heart was ripped apart, as Ellie had just figured it out. She was just a one night flavor for Strider, nothing special to him. At that moment, the burn built her character into the Road Queen, the defiance and rage escalated beyond comprehension, no guy would want to see this. Not even Ellie could have predicted what this would do to her soul. It became a twenty year driver. Yet in spite of the all this, she blew off the early warning label until a couple of months later, for now she easily traded fun time for a heart ache.

Ellie tore down Highway 77 on her way back to the Cinnamon House when the cave spirits entered her car. A rush of cold musty wind entered the driver's window, knocking her head down on the steering wheel. Something had gripped the wheel as if she had hit ice, but this was June. The Mustang went into a 360 spin, one after another, totally out of control. After spinning into three 360s, she took her foot off the gas and the car shut down in a green grass ditch. Ellie got out of the car and walked several miles to call a wrecker. Two days later, the mechanic said there was nothing wrong with the car, but what had happened to you?

CHAPTER 3

SPIRIT OF DIVISION

In July, Ellie traveled to Stony Lake Park, just thirty miles east of the Cinnamon House. With tears streaming down her cheeks, Ellie sunk on a wooden swing and gazed out over the white sandy beach full of babies and toddlers. She clenched the rusty chain to swing back and forth to dry the tears. What did she do wrong? It took decades for her to realize that fear fuels men's souls, fear of commitment, she didn't buy that Strider didn't love her, so why the abandonment?

She swung back and forth and watched the calm summer lake clouds gather in a circle above a legendary sunken site. While on the swing Ellie began to receive images of the underwater site. She knew there was a stone building, a black Bear Mound and a long stone pier all sunken long ago. On the beach's edge, she caught a glimpse of a young boy laughing at an object splashing in the waves. She had heard there was a whole city underwater, something which she would discover later on. But right now she was trying to figure out testosterone, why do guys have to fool around and why did she always forgive them?

Purity, loyalty, and an unsure totality, were they traded for pleasure? No, that wasn't it. Ellie recalled four weeks earlier, in June, the first colors ever placed on Ellie's back were Strider's. Even if was only for a moment outside of Louie's Bar. The dark blue denim jacket, with cut off sleeves, had red and yellow patches on the back that shouted out the Ancient Valley's name. This was the greatest prize of her life; color meant more than marriage to her. Ellie started crying, but didn't want Strider to see. Wearing cut off short shorts and spiked high heels, Ellie was in heaven. Yet, it only lasted an evening before they were gone, so the Road Queen emerged. It was always that contrast with Ellie, one moment of incredible bliss, the next the let down on the sidewalk.

Ellie never could see past the colors, the great prize until years later, and even then she still wanted them, more than diamonds or gold. She would fly several sets of colors in her time. Colors were not power to her, but more of an alliance of complexity, after all 100 guys would back and load you up at anytime, or so she thought. The red and yellow warrior shouted out against the contrasting club's colors. What fun.

In late June, Ellie recalled driving down to Beeville on a roll. Smothered in kisses and colors, then suddenly Strider was driving her up to the quarry where tons of white gravel had been crushed in front of the ancient water baby spring. Ellie could see them dancing. She believed in water babies, but her mind was going blank, once again, kissing on the back of that bike. Water babies gurgled, as the kissing would not stop.

Strider passed out again, this time back in town, in the upstairs of the old feed store, because he was exhausted. Ellie woke up to see Bear Man standing at the head of the couch with a big smiling face. He was hitting on her.

Emitting pure chemo electricity, Bear Man was equally radiant, long blonde hair and shimmering blue eyes. He explained "Ellie, you just don't see it. Strider's too high, he can never understand you. He has so many other girls, he just don't care about you. I would never treat you like that. I would give anything to be with you, so please give me a chance."

Bear Man's soft cheek was resting on hers, trying to steal a kiss, he caressed her cheek, his eyes locked on hers, longing to kiss her, but no. Ellie stood firm and remained loyal to Strider. Bear Man, how many times, years later, would she think of that guy. What would of happened, had she taken that chance. Soon after that June evening, Bear Man fell from great heights, dying before he could live, once again leaving Strider to carry the torch. His death drove Strider deeper into his own gloom.

Suddenly Strider woke up, his mood was sour and restless, when he stormed out the door, down the steps and to the bar. He totally ignored her, like a toy he had already tired playing with her. This was the real shock, because Ellie still couldn't get it. She felt he was lying to himself, because she knew how bad he wanted her, so this was a lie. Later, she discovered she was living an illusion, because if he were capable of loving anyone beyond himself, he would have been there for her. But right now, he was larger than life to Ellie, the best and only one for her, so why was she in so much pain all the time? She was tempted, burned and loyal to the wrong guy, it happened all the time.

Rejected once again, she tried to revive herself, to comprehend the last event that had burned her so badly. Strider never returned that one particular June evening, so a great rift grew between them. Strider had pursued the younger ideal. Elli was torn, shaken and determined to do better, to conquer more than possible. So she headed back down to the Clubhouse, looking for Thor, to harden her soul, creating an inner strength, a later discipline based on the get-back theory.

It was another Friday night ride on the jack of spades corner, 150 bikes roar endlessly in from nowhere. Waiting for new boys, 151 rum and the pool table. The Clubhouse filled with black leather, smoke and beer. Enter Thor, just what she had needed, no solidity, no solution, just more trouble. The smoke stained wooden floors tilted towards the Lake. Supported by wooden beams that were equally bent, the place contained a great celebrating spirit, a joyous mood of discovery, a place where the anticipation turned into reality. The place had always attracted the restless explorers. Sex was opened up in the backyard and upstairs, downstairs, any where... It was a real tripping biker bar. Yet, Ellie maintained her dignity, in some form.

The pool table was covered in ancient emerald green. It smelled of spilled beer and leather.

Ellie put up her quarter, her main focus was to kick as much ass as she could that evening. Actually, it was a metaphor, a method for an early power struggle, after all who really wins? Thor would always win. Yet, somehow the dreams were dissolving quickly, so change was inevitable.

Following the July swing set reflections, Ellie returned to the Cinnamon House to escape the pain and focus on color. Ellie chose another path, she moved from biker colors to glass. She decided to make stained glass windows to record the visual events and explain her story. Her first mechanical piece was a Harley Sportster cam shaft drive gear window (Figure 1). It was in honor of Strider's 1969 black and chrome Sportster and their first ride out. The image had 28 quartz crystal inlays, combined with a large Arkansas stone, one of the Yu Chi stones, found near Spiro Mounds, Oklahoma. The stones were a gift from her friends. They contained inspirational rainbows locked inside of them, especially the large center crystal.

Already Ellie had fused ancient with current events. This would make up for the pain, just journey onwards, she thought, really just to the ancient past. When Ellie made the Sportster stained glass window she could hear the camshaft twirling, projecting a torrid iridescent light shower on the floor. It spun light over the ruins of her lost alliances. But, alas, it was just a Sportster. It was the Sportster stained glass window sale that got her enough cash to buy her first bike, a 1972 HD Superglide.

However, by early September, Ellie still had haunting Stony Lake images on her mind. They increased in sound and color every day and night. These were the days before salvation, when Ellie had no concept of the Holy Spirit, just images of ancient skies.

There was only one teacher she knew who could understand these objects and images, as he had been diving at Stony Lake, so Ellie went to meet the famed archeologist, Dr. Soren. The preparation for the first journey included anointing the forehead with olive oil and rosemary scent which filled the air. They met in an isolated glen, just north of Stony Lake, adjacent to a large bolder called Spirit Rock.

The Spirit Rock bolder resembled a 20 foot meteor. Composed of gray granite, ribbed with darkened compression marks, it pulsed along with the chirping frogs. It was as though it was floating on top of another world. Spirit Rock was where the frogs sang and the worlds open. Ellie could see the different portals to the universe from this place. The site so greatly impressed her that later she fused and soldered a Spirit Rock world in glass.

The Spirit Rock window recorded the miraculous opening of the Phi time bridge, as it appeared in the amber sky (Figure 2). Phi was an abstract number, found in the golden mean and a universal life force with in all things. The Phi bridge that helped open and close the portals of time and space so the star ships could travel. The window recorded an ancient time when the moon was conjunct with the sun, in Gemini to the trickster Venus, as the 19th dimension opened its portal to Orion's belt. This event had been recorded in a classic Mayan codex and was pictured in the window that reflected three global realms.

Solstice again, she thought, she had heard the frogs chirping, but also recalled the distant drum beats sounding out harmonic seven notes, followed by a syncopated eighth note. Twins arose in her spirit, allowing the duality of nature's secret mysteries to fly out of the Thunderbird Mounds. Twin orange thunderbirds rose out of the red battlefield above the purple rock wall that divided the subterranean chamber and the green seas of time. The orange fall trees and yellow moon above the inner tribunal chamber were engulfed in the turquoise sky.

In the center earth area, a green spring, tribunal council and a cobalt blue waterfall penetrated the layers of heaven and earth. The division of realms reminded Ellie of the story of Lazarus and the rich man. In Luke 16, the rich man gazes across the great gulf between purgatory and paradise, his heart longing for Abraham's comfort. The rich man longs for a drop of water but cannot reach across purgatory to heaven. So it was with the ancient layered world of causation, once an action had been initiated, it had to play out to completion. The triple realms remained individually impenetrable.

In the Spirit Rock window, just below the moss and turquoise blue light, a Stonehenge portal recorded a yellow orange sunrise. Under this world, close to the Mayan ball court, the stone council ring was placed near the spring. A triangular stone table had been assembled for the exchange of peace treaties and trinkets. It was a miniature mid-western Stonehenge that recorded the legends of the Three Nations.

After the Spirit Rock visit, later that afternoon, Dr. Soren took her to Stony Lake and told her the site's secrets of the underwater crystal lodge. It was called the Temple of the

Sun and was sunken long ago. It was the building she had seen in her dreams. Learning about the sunken Lodge of Warriors, myths and legends allowed Ellie to make comparisons to her own imagination. These things happily presented her with an explanation of her world. This journey to Spirit Rock and Stony Lake had answered, no, aligned many questions, turning jumbled painful thoughts into incredible images. Would Dr. Soren remember or even allow this? Ellie didn't say a word to him about the images. She would draw, paint and fuse them later on.

Ellie could clearly recall the before days, when stone circles where important, when drums, light beams and songs called the distant fire ships to earth. When the Phi Bridge opened and closed galactic portals, allowing the crystal ships' space travel. It was a time when all elements radiated in harmony in the days before the great flood.

In the past, just as now, something had gone amiss. After the ancients built their seven Temples up and down the Mississippi, Missouri and St. Lawrence Rivers, the great crystal Temples were sunken under the sea. So the Elders hid their building equipment, devices, knowledge and treasures in seven sealed caves near the rivers. The seven crystal temples were then flooded, their songs, colors and vibrations had sunken in the lakes, only to be hidden until the Final Days of Glory. Could the seven Temples be the Biblical seven lamps that once illuminated the earth?

In late September, after completing the Spirit Rock window, Ellie got on her Glide and rode to Stony Lake. She went to the park and got on her favorite swing. She had been introduced to something terrific, very fantastic, because she could see beneath the water and recall inside one of the sunken structures. Ellie was trying to make sense of all this and that is why she decided to record the images in watercolor, pencil and glass.

While on the swing, and peering into the lake, Ellie glanced down and saw a small, silver metal object under the swing set pole. It looked like a gas cap, so she paused to pick it up. The circular cap was topped with a large silver triangle combined with two brass indentations. The triangle rested on a raised octagonal platform. It reminded her of a gear puller. What a strange thing to find at a playground, thought Ellie. Little did she realize that this silver key was in its first shape-shifting phase designed to define her future. It would also unlock ancient pathways to decode future events.

This trip to Stony Lake helped Ellie gather her past and present life images. Ellie forgot about crying for Strider and wanted to draw, paint and cut out the glass images of her ideas. She got on her new Glide and road around the ancient Lake. Ellie watched the clouds form in rings above the underwater structure. The Lake held the Temple of the Sun, Moon and a Bear pyramid, the one that contained the ancient records. Why could she see these things underneath the water?

Strange how that site would pull her out of biker pain. A longing to pursue a tranquility, a soft feminine image was being restructured within her. After years of being discarded, thrown away like a rag doll, Stony Lake proved to be a pivoting point. Ellie saw a futuristic image, which sent her to the library searching the rarest books on earth for answers. Learning nine languages, she immersed herself in ancient dynasties. Her soul was torn, divided between starving for love or for knowledge. Although craving the Clubhouse boy toy freedom, Ellie changed her direction as she decided to fuel her knowledge.

Next Ellie journeyed to Spider Mountain Park to visit with the Rock Elders. Nestled in the black bear cave, near the cliff's edge, she communed with the Elders. She gained enough courage to go to the twin brother's platform and obtain the following great ideas.

CHAPTER 4

RIDING FREE

Spider Mountain Park, 50 miles northwest of Stony Lake, was the home of Winnebago creation. It was the home of Sacred Lake, the ancient warrior initiation site. Rock towers ascended high above Sacred Lake. It was the only place where Ellie could see an original creation myth, acted out as it had happened during a startling shape-shifting event. After climbing up the steep rocky trail to the platform, she viewed the soaring eagles circling over the blue-green water.

Ellie climbed up to the twin rock towers to speak with the Elders. They often spoke to her from the platform in front of the Spider Mountain twin cliffs. The broad shouldered towers were like two consoling brothers. When Ellie turned to catch her breath, there was a yellow, pink and purple sky, a chromatic brilliant glow, which reflected the dawn of creation, and she giggled.

Ellie was so distracted by the chromatic light show that she looked down over the rocks and viewed the pure crystal springs empting into Sacred Lake, located ninety stories below her. Ellie followed the ripples of the underwater springs to the Lake's center where water spouts began to swirl. Next, over twenty water jets sprouted up and down like the bubbler at the zoo. The small water tornadoes spurted up towards the cliffs. Little did she know that amorphous beings would rise out of the water jets.

Suddenly, following a series of falling blue grey parallel plane light shafts, without warning, a Scythe dragon emerged, out of the blue ice crystal water. It was a yellow and red scaly creature with folded green wings (Figure 3). It spewed forth foam and was shrieking horribly. The Water Dragon rose thirty feet above Sacred Lake's surface, gnawing and thrusting at the empty sky. The sounds of its screams were something Ellie had never heard before they were terrifying in agony, a death throw cry that pulsated through rocks, the echoes to be immortalized in time. The great Dragon spit jets of slime all over Sacred Lake. Ellie had read about this multi-dimensional presentation in a Winnebago myth book.

Just as she turned away, abruptly out of the thin, transparent orange, chromatic air, a huge blue, orange and purple Thunderbird appeared. Its purple tail feathers shot red flames towards the sky. Talons outstretched, it flew rapidly towards the creature. It didn't spit fire at the TBird, just slimy glue dribbled out of his mouth. Ellie watched as the massive bird clenched the beast, just behind its neck and torso. Tidal waves splashed towards the shore. The great TBird lifted the Dragon out of the Lake and then hurled him back into the deep water, with a big smacking belly flop. The Dragon reminded her of Revelation 13, the great beast that emerges out of the waters.

Four more Thunderbirds appeared from the corners of the earth. Prior to grabbing the dragon, the Thunderbirds had hurled rocks at the beast. The rock eggs were flung in elliptical patterns. They were propelled toward the dragon but had hit the southern cliffs. Eventually, they shook loose some of the hillside boulders, causing a gigantic rock slide. The hurled rocks caused a landslide that remained throughout the ages.

When Ellie glanced up into the pink and blue sky, she briefly saw the end of a fleet of crystal ships, above and to the right side of the largest shrieking Thunderbird. Natu-aka-seth, she thought in Sauk, the western land Thunderbird, on its course for the Milky Way. The elongated ships had triangular hulls that extended toward the earth. The fuselage was tapered with swan-shaped wings that were extended, gliding across the sky. The fleet of pink and purple crystal ships vanished as quickly as they appeared.

In the southern corner just beneath her, Ellie saw two large diamond crystal geodes rise out of the sandy shore and rotate with sparkling brilliance. Their many facets captured the sunlight and threw dazzling light speckles all over the water and shore. Just as quickly as it had emerged, the vision ended. Ellie realized she had been allowed to view the first Creation battle, one that never left her mind, but could only be exceeded by the next event. This was the land of pre-Cambrian sandstone wonders that stood within the oldest mountain range on earth.

Ellie recalled the Creation scene on her next visit to the Sacred Lake platform several weeks later with a new friend. Ellie's heart was pounding during a modeling event. There was Simon, Nikon in hand, yelling at her, what happened was she scared or was she just plain stupid? He sent her to the edge of a cliff, to pose for him and his magazine. Now she couldn't stand that guy, she just spent an evening with him and now he was screaming at her, calling her a liar. She couldn't model, because she was too close to the edge. Just as Simon angrily lunged towards her Ellie jumped out of reach, slipped on a red rock, and bumped her head. As Simon ran off in a rage, Ellie grabbed her head and collapsed on the platform. She closed her eyes and faded into yet another day dream.

It was during a golden yellow sunset, that she viewed Spider Mountain and Sacred Lake from above the ground, a bird's eye triple layer view of the future (Figure 4). While lying in a dream state, Ellie was distracted by a red cross that floated in the sky, then another, a yellow one and finally a huge gold cross. These were the days before salvation, so their true meaning had escaped her. A pearl white dragonfly with blue dotted wings glided past her.

In the bright yellow sky Ellie saw the pearl white dragonfly glide toward a double gateway of illusion. In the middle realm, a frisky, chrome orange and yellow puppy dragon galloped away from a stone ivory dolmen and raced towards a gold mine that had exploded with large nuggets. The melt down occurred under the great pyramid's eye of the Nine Caves and golden serpent.

Ellie learned later on that these images were found in Osirian creation myths.

The lower right underwater scene held a Bear Mound with a blue- tipped golden pyramid placed on its backside. The Bear Mound pyramid held hundreds of written tablets, copies of Egypt's Alexandrian records. The tablets describe pre-flood records and prophecy. The Bear faced towards his footsteps that led back to the underwater trinket cave. Inside the cave was a great meeting, the union of warriors representing three nations. Judging from the red and yellow rays, they were brainstorming about future events. It was the Three Nation merger of mid-western tribes.

Next, the blue-white dragonfly evolved out of the third dimensional portal and dropped a silver object near Ellie's reclining torso. Startled, Ellie awoke when it landed with a thud next to her left side. She reached across the white diamond sand that dusted the stony platform, to grasp the silver circle. This time it looked different, radiating a brass tinge as it reflected the sunset's golden rays. It was smaller, shinier than the last time she saw it at the Stony Lake swing set.

Although the triangle was larger, and embossed with circular patterns, and incised with intricate floral designs, the brass circles were encased with silver wrought figure eight designs. Once again, the triangle rested on top of an octagon, but now the base rested on a notched gear. It resembled the cog under the harmonic gear puller of her '65 Mustang. So just what was this thing that had re-emerged from ancient dreams into her reality? At that time, Ellie did not understand that the vision was the object that would tie the past to the future. Desiring a change of scenery, and a possible explanation, Ellie chose to return to Stony Lake. She had to return to the swing set were she first saw the silver gas cap thing.

CHAPTER 5

ANCIENT EDUCATION: INSIDE THE TEMPLE

Ellie knew she had to return to Stony Lake where, under the spring fed water, lay the Temple of the Sun that contained the great council chamber that held the arena of change (Figure 5). She had seen it before, when she was at the swing set crying for Strider. Under the green pea soup water, filled with farm run off that fueled the algae growth, sat the Temple of the Sun, partly embedded in the muck. It was in a time portal, one that opened and closed only occasionally, and those who were not supposed to peer inside, could or would not. It was protected by the water babies and Ellie believed if you couldn't remember them or believe in them, you would not see the Temple of the Sun. The images had intensified in her mind after she had visited with Dr. Soren. Ellie sat on the north shore beach and gazed into the water.

The Temple of the Sun was built on top of a cross-shaped notched structure. The complete site was 70 feet under water. It was composed of three layers, but the fused glass window only revealed the Temple as one unit. The base had a notch in the southwestern corner.

The flat top pyramidal Temple had a 120' square base and was topped with an additional small truncated pyramid. The tiny top pyramid had a second tier, a bench or porch. After irrigation and partial Temple submersion, ions ago, the bench was used as a pier. One could canoe up to it, as it had been built along the artificial river.

Now, the Temple lay partly submerged in mud on Stony Lake's floor, adjacent to the Bear Mound and Turtle and Conical rock structures. Directly across from the Temple of the Sun was a tall pointed tower.

The Temple of the Sun's base had a 100 foot corridor extended from the dry inner chamber. Three other rooms and the corridor radiated from the Temple's base. Painted on the corridor and room's stucco beige walls were vases full of peacock feathers, straw wisps and images of dancing black bears that were oddly combined tropical green and plumed red birds. It was a union of Native American and Aztec images.

The inner chamber contained a round hollow stone table that floated on a circular ring. Around the table were twelve triangular-shaped stone stools each balancing on three legs. It was a council ring.

In the table's center lay a ring of twelve stones. They appeared to be faceted like diamonds, but reflected only turquoise and cobalt blue light. The twelve stones floated around a hollow circle in the center of the table. In the stone ring's center was a many tongued flame that burned endlessly into the night. Ellie gazed at the orange and red flames that lapped at the stale, musty chamber air. The flames did not appear to be housed or contained, but just burned forever, alighting above a hollow space in the stone's center. Ellie glanced underneath the flames' core into an inner white diamond light.

The brilliant light radiated spherically, reaching far down to the earth's core while it systematically spun like dancing diamonds under the flame. Ellie stared deeply into this eternal flame. Its hypnotic, luminescent power recalled the glory of the Lord's descending throne, found in St. John's Revelation 4:3 & 5. The Lord sat on a jasper and sardius throne, glowing from the waist up, from which proceeded lightening, thunder and voices. The seven lamps of fire burned before the throne, which are the seven spirits of God. Could this site be one of those lamps?

The flame's orange and blue tongue created hypnotic shadows on the hand hewn limestone walls. Flickering like a red and yellow bonfire, a hint of blue skirted the edges. The intensity of the flame recalled Ezekiel 1:27, where he saw the Lord from the waist up, looking like glowing metal, like fire, surrounded in a brilliant light. The flame's intensity rang out prophetic fulfillment. Could this be the Biblical Holy Spirit's eternal flame or Egypt's Osirian original council chamber? Ellie was inside the Temple of the Sun, gazing mindlessly towards yet another tomorrow when a new vision emerged (Figure 6). This time the Temple of the Sun was rising from the Lake. Venus burned brightly in the silver sky, when suddenly a great earth tremor distracted her thoughts. It was very alarming, as if the earth had been shaken from deep within the core. Suddenly, the earth tipped, Ellie saw it slip, dip and turn six degrees on its axis in an instant. Large amounts of water poured out of Stony Lake, as the Temple rose, and flooded the land.

It was the day after Christmas, when rivers and waves of water were propelled into gigantic mountain ranges creating a cataclysmic tidal wave. The apocalyptic tsnami was louder than thunder. Streams of blue and yellow, silver light emerged from the rising Temple of the Sun, as it rose like a beacon on the horizon. The four Thunderbirds flew over to view the event. An underwater panther churned in the deep, thrashing hideously in an awkward joyous celebration. The churning panther had a friend, a recoiled Dragon who awoke behind a stone wall, amidst the chaos of the north shore waters. Although it was like a Tibetan Bardo state, the animals' actions paralleled St. John's Revelation 6:12-14. The great red Dragon had been awakened. Following the blowing winds, an earthquake, the sun blackened, the moon turned red and the sky rolled up. Things had been shaken and awakened on earth.

However, just as quickly as the future image rang aloud in her mind, another more pressing presence entered the room. The vision faded when a slender powerful force entered the council chamber, where Ellie was now standing. It was Atun Khonsu, the Sun-Moon King and the Keeper of the True Eternal Flame. He had been waiting for Ellie patiently for 5000 years.

Atun Khonsu was the eternal youth, bemused by everything, not particularly caring about anything. He wore only a tan leather breach cloth decorated with hand sewn coral and turquoise stones on the belt. In his hand, he held a bow and arrow. It was more of a toy for him, much like everything else he used.

Ellie remembered when she first saw him from above Stony Lake, on the swing, looking back in time. He was sitting cross-legged on top of the Temple of the Sun, sort of bemused at her crying intervention. He got up and strode across the top of the structure with graceful strides and a smile.

He was laughing at her struggles and was tossing red candy crystals to a little jeweled dragon. Atun Khonsu was an eternal youth and he had not aged since their first acquaintance, in the past age. Ellie had also seen him sitting on truncated Temple top bench, with his head in his hand, resting while looking down at the stream, as in the before days.

But now he was standing right next to her, she could feel his presence permeate entirely through her body as if was merging, amalgamating into, through and piercing her soul. God, this is a strong one, Ellie thought, but how to push him out and did she really want too?

Ellie more than remembered his kisses from the before days, the pure joy and later pain was too strong even from 5,000 years ago. She savored his presence, and recalled his effect upon her heart, soul and body and subsequent complete abandonment. Would she ever go back to that intense bliss for another 5000 year rejection? It was just like Strider only it had happened in the distant past and was viewed in the present age, but she knew she could still change the future.

Ellie pondered the idea of sharing her soul with an entity like that, and decided she had to ride free, for the moment. Still, there was something terribly important that he had to tell her. He stood behind her and placed his arms around her waist, she could feel his strength and endless energy.

Ellie was consumed by his presence. She glanced down at his hands with long tapering fingers, although so ethereal, there was no blood in these veins. Atun Khonsu was not alive in the flesh, but a true light being. As he gestured to the side hallway, she felt herself gliding to a small landing, a pylon ledge, where although it should have been underwater in her recent memory, they were now standing at the edge of a stone pier, the second bench step.

While ribbons of sweet green-blue water flowed past them, Ellie caught glimpses of white, blue and pink water lilies and lotuses twirling in the stream. Birds and crickets were chirping and a sweet delicate fragrance of myrrh filled the air. Ellie was not aware of anything but the stream, Atun Khonsu and the special effects when she felt his hand reach down to touch hers. He lifted her arm up into the air, about 90 degrees and gestured to an area in the river about 50 feet directly in front of her. He grasped her waist even tighter and placed his head on her shoulder, still gazing out into the waters, while permeating her soul. His hand dropped, as did Ellie's, as she watched a small swirl of water pull down under and the current change.

Suddenly the downward whirlpool collapsed, making a loud sucking noise, water spiraled into a funnel towards the deep bottom. After several moments, an 18 foot stone cone-shaped pillar began to rise out of the abyss. It was a tan tower, shaped like an obelisk, but instead of a capped pyramid top, it had a cylindrical tapering end composed of transparent rock crystal. Inside the crystal cylinder was a man's face, he had deep set eyes, a beard and appeared to be beaming into the current reality.

Ellie laughed whatever reality that maybe! The face could have been Christ's or some other great Elder. Ellie wondered what to do next, as the head appeared to be alive, aware inside the transparent cylinder, but was just bobbing about. Nothing was happening for several moments, when it occurred to her that this was some type of time-space portal. Manifestation between galaxies often took time to emerge, so she thought. Further, because of his serious expression and grizzly foreboding mood, Ellie thought perhaps she didn't want to stick around to see what would happen next.

As quickly as all the joy and warmth had flooded her mind, soul and body, Atun Khonsu vanished, leaving her ice cold. An even more chilling wind began to stir in the euphoric setting as if an ice age were about to set in. All the past live kisses were gone and the totality of her singleness was upon her. Ellie shook her head and looked down at her toes, what to do now she thought. She closed her eyes very tightly and wondered about the silver key and what did she do for Jesus today?

When Ellie awoke she was lying on the north beach near the Stony Lake boathouse. Now it was fall, as she looked about at the orange and red sugar maples and shuddered as she felt the October chill in the air. The sun was going down as she sat up slowly, rather dazed from the last vision. It concerned her greatly as the vivid scenes were draining her.

Physically exhausted, Ellie entered an unlocked boat house looking for a coat. There in the cobwebbed corner, in a broken pile, were the remnants of her previously lost Glyph Letter window (Figure 7). The Glyph Letter window instantly gave her a newly detailed, yet recognizable, message. Ellie brought it out of the corner and examined it at length. She wondered how her window ended up in the boathouse. There were four rows of symbols, ancient glyphs, divided by different colored backgrounds. Reading from left to right, the first bottom row contained a large golden orb and setting sun placed in a blue boat. Ellie had seen similar solar barks in Egyptian paintings from the Rameseum. Following her first impression of the "Solar Boats" she mumbled "Oh no." Ramses II and Ramses III, the 1280 B.C. list goes on for generations.

Her eyes followed the gold zigzag path to a blown apart gray orb depicting Spirit Rock in the red background. In the corner, a strange glyph resembled a backward F. Ellie recognized it as Phoenician. The next row held another glyph and a half Phi bridge; the small blue arced gateway inside the circular portal depicted another Sky Bridge.It was a portal, a time warp tunnel, in the turquoise sky. She looked closely at the portal representing a bridge across time, solar system and galaxy. The blue Phi bridge could take a soul from earth to the Pleiades, Sirius, Lyra or Orion's Belt without a blink. The Glyph window was a stellar map, an ancient record that contained a future message. Then it dawned on her, she formed this window after a Big Cave stone slab she had seen while kissing Strider. Ellie recognized the forgotten romantic glyph source.

She continued to examine the letters recalling the Chinese Yu bear legend. Yu could hip, hop and jump across Orion's Belt. He could pull people in a star cart. The path of the Taoist Bear, Yu, danced across the Milky Way pulling and pushing time in his efforts to generate a time warp. A slip and slide to the 3rd row of glyphs that held a green arch, symbolizing a star ship loaded with people headed towards Lyra's purple sky.

Ellie had immersed herself in this ancient galactic fantasy, trying to read the map, while

Strider had pursued the younger long-legged blonde. These ladies were innumerable, but this one hurt more than the others.

Ellie hadn't seen him in months, but suddenly and simultaneously, Satan's dart pierced her heart beyond measure. How could she deflect that pain, the great sorrow of rejection, when she was still tied to him and could see, feel and taste all the action. The Bible says that God always will offer you a way out, by praising his Holy name and the dart would dissolve.

She couldn't have him now, so her mind returned to the galaxy of wonder. The final row contained a yellow globe or colonized planet, that was about to be transformed. Here the people would build the golden script temple of records.

The glyphic prophecy! The orbs suggested a triple planet line up for the sailing of the solar boats. The shape shifter of time and space appealed to Ellie. She deeply pondered the message of the three planet alignment. Was it a future or past event or both? The traveling of ancient star ships, created too many questions, but at least it tore her away from the pain. Ellie wondered what to do with the Glyph window so she left it in the boathouse. Ellie then knew she had to find the Big Cave, as the glyphs matched her memory of Strider's story.

Ellie strolled out of the boathouse into the chilly air. She glanced back and saw tiny green orbs flowing out of the center of Stony Lake. They rose like tiny fish bubbles and floated across the Lake's smooth surface. They glided north towards a woodland trail, which later she discovered lead to Golden Creek Cave. This was a second holding site, yet another untold story.

While enjoying the bubbles and thinking about Atun Khonsu, Ellie got on her 1972 Superglide HD. The bike fired up too slow. It spit and shook, but it started. After she rode a few miles, suddenly the bike was smoking and shaking. "Ah oh!" too hot she thought, it had fired up too high on TDC, top dead center. Then BAM, she hit a big pot hole, and the bike began to shake violently.

The front end started to lift up then slammed down as the bike began to wobble. She was sure the rim was bent, when suddenly the engine began to rev up more than necessary. It almost hit full throttle, so she squeezed the clutch in, as the overloaded cylinders roared.

The bike began to spit more white smoke as Ellie slid off the road and shut it down on the blacktop. As it was over heating, she dismounted the sled and spun the front wheel. She noticed a bent rim which explained the front end shudder.

She looked at the scorched metal cylinder and saw the tell tale oil marks, the source of the white smoke and laughed. It's all smoke and mirrors anyways, she thought. Now at the mercy of the road, Ellie wouldn't leave her bike. Still stunned, she held up her bike and waited for a passerby. Ellie reflected upon the road's emptiness, the glyphic window and Temple vision. The bike, visions and cylinders were too new to be this hot.

Squirrels chattered under the nearby maple tree, so she placed the bike on the kick stand and walked over towards them. She kicked the red, yellow and orange leaves to startle and chase the critters away. Still pissed off, she thought about placing her finger on the boiling hot cylinder, but she already knew only time could cool it down.

Ellie sat down under the sugar maple and sighed. She knew she'd fire it up again but still not a soul had passed by. Yet, she liked the theatre of the absurd, being stranded. It was the kick of the vulnerable unknown, she was subject to the elements. After all, she was probably more out of control than any of the biker boys.

Propped up against the sugar maple tree, Ellie closed her eyes and began to dream about the mystery boys in her life when another spell hit her hard. Now those haunting swirling waters were sinking the Temple, this time it was not rising. When it was sinking, the blue water splashed white caps on the Temple's limestone walls. The four dragons were thrashing in the waves and were being pulled down into a pit. She could see the waves, feel the chill and smell the seaweed lake water.

Suddenly, thunk, oh no, the bike had toppled over on its side, awakening her from the day dream. Ellie opened her eyes and saw the sled on its side. How could she lift those 640 lbs? Ellie walked over to the bike to where the sun had melted the black top under the kickstand. She caught a glimpse of a shiny silver object lying on the road, but as she stared at it, it rose from the pavement and spun in mid air. What a strange thing! Illusionary heat waves rose from the pavement, even though it was chilly, when her eyes were drawn to the silver circle. Ellie ran across the road to discover the silver key floating in space about two inches off the road.

How odd, she thought, a floater. Ellie had read about these objects in Egyptian magic books. Believing it to be hot, she grabbed her sleeve to grasp the object. It was cold and repelled from her hand like a magnet. It pushed against her palm and began to spin counter clockwise. How strange, she thought as she walked back to her bike, object in hand. When she placed the silver key on the tank, it suddenly lifted up and propped the bike up on to the kickstand. It then jumped back about two feet and dropped next to her.

Ellie was pleased as she looked down to view the silver key. Its shape recalled the gear puller, but now there was something more. The two indentations on the silver top were filled in with red glass. There were figure eight shaped looping patterns on the circle's edge that were filled with blue glass. The red and blue glass pieces found in the Glyph window reminded her of images from Strider's Cave. The strong visual link was formed from images she had seen when Strider had described the Big Cave. Even though this confirmed her need to return to Beeville, she thought about it for a while, then got on her bike and rode away. The Clubhouse had a stronger call.

On her ride, Ellie thought of all the mystery men in her life, it was Atun Khonsu that kept calling her back. The eternal youth continuously called her to Stony Lake and she loved that creature. He was a light dancing iceberg that radiated testosterone. Not fair, she thought, he would never die, nor age. Yet she would transform, he could not. He was stuck in the Temple until

Judgment Day, able to view all the seasons of many lives.

Ellie had to peer across time, gaze back into the purple veil, through a crimson mist of tears and sorrow, to remember him. This one was so strong, unbounded, determined and aloof. In the before days, her every breath, thought action and color was absorbed by him. If he wanted her beyond all realms of time, he wouldn't let her know. But she did know, she had figured it out 'cause he kept coming back. He came back for her friendship, not her heart, which pissed her off. She didn't know how, but one day this time, they would get it right.

Ellie recalled the good times with Atun Kkonsu. It was almost 5000 years earlier, when they exchanged deep secret treasures on the cliff edge, near the gurgling springs, which were carved above the cliffs west of the Spider Mountain towers (Figure 8). The cliff glyphs were the same as today's hearts and love poems. Only these glyphs were carved in gray granite, now filled in with green moss and yellow lichen. Of course, the poems were preserved in an illustrative baroque calligraphic script. They told of their love in multiple realms and passions.

It was another life time, when they joined hands together on the great mossy tower rock, dangled their feet over the edge and hurled stones into the brook that gurgled up from under the stoic elm tree. Twin moons and triple planets blended into the pink orange sunset. This was the past, but it also could be the newly revised future.

Laughing, smiling, telling secrets and promising all of their tomorrows, they merged their hearts forever. Dual deep green eyes and an embrace that would not let go, he held her in his arms so tenderly. Ellie had never known this, she fit so perfectly. But that was then and this was now. Ellie had moved on, in solitude, after he left her. Don't look back, she thought, you can't hold your breath. Ride, live and move on.

CHAPTER 6

TRUE VISION

Ellie looked up from her daydreaming as the bike glided back down to the Clubhouse. The ancient one had already consumed too much of her time. Back downtown to the rumble house on the wings of the blue hawk, she mused. As Ellie entered the Clubhouse, there was yet another dreamboat bad boy. Yet this time she felt the word of God telling her to be true, to turn from the black leather muscle boys to another light. So she put a hold on the guys. Her adamant loyalty made her different than the others. Her conviction, her faith in the unseen Miracle that God had waiting for her. She had waited a life time for the ethereal versus the real world. It was so difficult. She preferred the dream world, less pain.

Christ had called her to his glory at dawn, but by midnight the freedom ride was too strong, the comfort, the temporary friends, the beer, the jokes.... How many times had she gone back? Now it was Tuesday night and the roller girls cruised into the club of tattooed leather boys with eye, nose and mouth earrings. Ellie was back at the clubhouse with the ringnosed 20 year olds sousing in beer, girls and Jaeger shots. The crack of the eight ball rack broke the Tuesday night silence; overgrown kids on an overgrown romance.

Back at the Clubhouse what dreams unfolded? Drunks were describing their heroic acts; carburetors ripped open again, 2 or 4 jets, mixed with laughter and tequila shots. More interesting were those starters, the tight copper windings on a rounded steel shaft, the brushes, two flaring brushes, spring loaded and delicate winding springs. When they jammed, it gave Prestolite or Hitachi a fortune. Or more pointedly, a field short in the sealed armature, detectable only by centrifugal force, gave way around the copper breakage. So hey, soak that puppy in creosote, it'll seal her up! How many starters had she baked, to save the boys' money?

Exhausted from the ride, Ellie skipped outside to rest by her bike. She looked into the black sky to see the shimmering white diamond stars. After rolling back down to the Clubhouse where the anticipation was greater than the action, Ellie now knew she had to go to the Big Cave. She sighed as it was like crawling into a big black hole of rejection. The Valley held too many memories. The very next morning she took off to Strider's site outside of Beeville.

After the 40 mile descent into the Ancient Valley, Ellie stopped by the underground springs, west of the quarry, by the water baby bridge, to pick spring flowers, when she came across an alternate cave entrance. While gathering purple violets and lilies of the valley, she saw blue orbs streaming from out of the bog, from behind a waterfall, which hid the long lost Big Cave opening. The blue orbs reminded her of blow bubbles, only these eight inch iridescent orbs held tiny gold faces inside of them. They contained fairy faces that Ellie had read about in her water baby book. Several dozen orbs floated out of the cave, from under the waterfall, across the springs, and immediately disappeared into the dawn. Ellie was actually enjoying the bubbly, bouncy transfiguration, but doubted its longevity. Oh, the impermanence of all things, she noted.

Ellie tip toed down the creek's edge and peered into a bog and waterfall. She strode across three stones to stand underneath the waterfall. There, hidden behind a maze of vertical stone slabs, was another entrance to the Big Cave. It was a place that hadn't changed in ions of time. Ellie walked through the geometric maze and up a long stucco corridor. It was decorated with brown Celtic glyphs and gold Phoenician script. She turned left and ascended across a gateway. It's alright she thought, it's a water baby place. Beyond the corridor were three chambers.

The first chamber was filled with tools and tablets. It was the Tool Room for the Hall of Records, where tablets were made in dark brown streaky stone. The room was filled with half-finished tablets covered with incised glyphs, scribbles, darts and dashes that resembled her Glyph Letter window. Dozens of stone tablets written in some type of ancient early script or hieroglyphics, covering a time span of two thousand years, all in one room. This didn't make sense. Tablets dated 2850 B.C. where strewn about the porous floor with those from 300 A.D. Could the Big Cave been in use this long? The porous floor looked like bone china, lava that had been frozen in an instant.

Blue stalactites rose throughout the stone record chamber, under their base were circular rings of orange, yellow lights, their intensity oscillated in time and space. Cobalt and turquoise blue stalactites and stalagmites rose in layers throughout the cave. This 30' x 60' quagmire of dripped rock illuminated an open arena. Across the cavern the rock gleamed like orange and red columns. By the stone records were mallets and chisels.

Ellie noticed a sharp inclination towards a distant corner. Running across the dark musty room, Ellie entered the Library, where hundreds of carved stone slabs were stacked in rows. They were the ancient East-West records. The glyphs were pre-Atlantean, replicating the lost Alexandrian records. The tablets were lined up like dominoes.

Ellie felt awesomely blessed. She had been driven to so many extremes and now, once again, here was her reward. The tombstone tablets reminded her of fake toast in a toaster toy she had played with as a child. The pink toaster had blue and tan plastic toast that resembled the tablets, which made her laugh. The strange glyphs made her laugh because although she couldn't read them, she knew they held important information.

A narrow staircase in the front of the Library led downstairs to the adjacent Elder Room (Figure 9). Here were the great petrified statues of the long robed priests. They were carved in stone, yet copper formed replicas were intermingled among them. They appeared to be much older, yet ageless as their facial expressions were immutable, in constant transition. Bearded, pensive, alert, their eyes fixed downward upon the tablets, and a huge boulder. The frozen figures stood in front of a large stone cocoon that was composed of multicolored quartz rock crystal. It was blue, topaz and curved towards the ceiling.

Ellie then noticed a steep spiral ramp to the right of the cocoon. She descended several stories down the ramp into the final chamber called the Fire Crystal Room (Figure 10). This subterranean chamber housed a large wooden and gold box which held the orange-red fire crystals. These were the stones that had fueled the star ships long ago. They had been hidden and lay dormant for centuries. Soon, something will shake and awake the fire stones. Were they placed in the box by the blue spotted tail people from the Eastern Land? These were the people who knew how to revive the speaking stones with songs, light and dance. Or were these stones keys to Egyptian, Mayan or Atlantean records? Everything was once a ceremony with the Ancient ones!

Ellie stared at the gold wooden box and noticed it had a lock or insert place near the top.

It was decorated with a silver figure eight design with bits of red and blue inlayed glass. Recognizing the lock's indented pattern, Ellie knew she had to go back to Stony Lake to get the silver key and open the golden box. It was universal chore. So Ellie ran up the spiral ramp, through the Elder Room and Library, back down to the Tool Room and down the long corridor to go out the back entrance.

Ellie fired up the Superglide and raced 90 miles back to Stony Lake on that October day. There, by the swing set, as if waiting for her, was the stacked silver key gear puller. She felt like throwing it in the Lake, because she was so sick of this stuff and all the guys. She paused to swing a few times and then put the silver object in her pocket. It seemed six hours later when Ellie arrived at the water baby springs, although months had passed. She went through the alternative entrance and directly into the Fire Crystal chamber. She grasped the silver key from her belt and paused for a moment.

Ellie knelt by the golden wooden box that held the fire crystals, in Chamber Three, and stuck in the silver key. She hadn't taken the time to read the mystic glyphs, she just clicked the silver key a quarter turn to the right and a large stone slab slid open on the floor underneath the Fire Crystal box. This was just like Ellie, so caught up in the action that she forgot to read the instructions. The stone slab opened to reveal a large canal beneath her and suddenly water began to flood the room. The system of underground springs, which were controlled by ancient locks and gates, had been activated.

However, Ellie was distracted, surprised by what she saw inside the box. Here were red, orange and yellow diamond crystal geodes. Their grapefruit size impressed her. She grabbed one of the stones but then dropped it, due to its intense heat and quickly stood up in the musty cavern. The floor began to tremble and another slab dropped out from the side of the wall.

Nearly a dozen scrolls fell out on to the cavern floor. They were tightly bound and sealed with a red wax seal. The floor was shaking even more violently, but Ellie quickly grabbed one of the parchment scrolls because she had wanted to look at the glyphs. Just as she touched the scroll, the rushing water poured into the back cavern and the floor became unstable. Ellie tossed the scroll back into the pile and ran really fast out of the chamber, up the spiral ramp. Her mind raced forward as she had wanted to collect the information and examine the artifacts, but there was no time, so she continued to climb out of the cave.

Unknown to Ellie, when she first opened the golden wooden box, before she took a crystal out, a light beam poured from box to the ceiling, and returned into the box's bottom. More light beams lit the ceiling like a diamond and penetrated far beyond that. Some of the light rays beamed through the cave's ceiling, up into the sky, through the solar system, deep into distant galaxies and penetrated a black hole. Then suddenly, a silver light beam bounced back to the earth, which would eventually cause the great globe to shake, wobble and tip on its side. The opening of the wooden box had accelerated time and an irreversible sequence of complex events.

As the Big Cave channel lock was opened and the Fire Crystal Chamber began to fill with water, miles away, the Stony Lake Temple pyramid began to rise. The water drained out of Stony Lake through a series of 90 mile long underground pressurized stone-gated channels. Water began to cover the land as the six degree tilt of the earth was about to fall into place.

Simultaneously, the rising Temple triggered the top platform tier to slide open and a rose-shaped crystal reaching toward the sky. As the flower crystal emerged out of the tiny truncated stone Temple formation it beamed a series of multi-colored lights into the sky, stirring the heavens with a northern lights show.

The kaleidoscope of beams signaled the six other sunken temples to rise. Each site had its mythic counter parts, including Sun and Moon, Peace and War Temple Pyramids, the Bear, Eagle and Dragon mounds. They were all ancient sites that held assorted records and awoke the earth to its new realm.

As Ellie was running down the hill towards her bike, she noticed the increase of flowers, fairies, water babies, talking dragonflies and other mystic creatures which were beginning to emerge. The critters danced in circles out of the tall green grasses. The water babies splashed on top of the sun sparkled pebbles. It was not such a terrible event, after all. It was wonderful, arriving in increased color, sound and stunning intensity.

CHAPTER 7

ROSE CRYSTAL RISING

Little did Ellie know that she had opened the canal lock which allowed the Temple of the Sun to rise. The silver object was the key of Knowledge and it had opened the canals to raise the rose quartz crystal (Figure 11). The large crystal, housed inside the truncated pyramid, began to unfold like a flower. As it emerged out of the slimy green seaweed, the red and pink crystal stone created large waves and beamed light rays into eternity and back. It pushed out of the truncated limestone pyramid top.

The great crystal had been entombed, housed in the limestone rock of the Temple of the Sun for ages. The water was churning tumultuously. It was suddenly the earth tilt day and its axis was shifting, slip sliding on its side six degrees, calling to the end of an age. As the large crystal water rose unfolded, it sent light beams and sparks to the sky, sun and beyond. It was one of seven ancient sites that all were beginning to rise out of the Mississippi and Missouri Rivers, including the distant Lake Superior, Huron and Erie. Each site held their secret artifacts and had individual specific directions.

So opened the crystal rose and with it arrived increased splendor and chaos. When the universe accelerates splendor, does chaos increase as well? Would the opening of time, the rise of the rose rock crystal accelerate these two opposing forces into tomorrow, or would their struggle drop to the side, as the tsunami waves rose in strength? If salvation had cancelled chaos, only cosmic splendor could be amplified.

That question was answered, indeed only in conjunction with twin stars rising in Gemini, it was very Mayan, Native American, Tibetan and Biblical. Ellie recalled the Dresden Codex prophecy and the Aztec wheel's layering of time. However, the ending of the great dilemma was not found in the texts or churning water. Beams from the rising seven temples lit the earth like seven pin-pointed lamp lights. Did the seven temples release the seven angels representing the seven Biblical lamps? Whatever the interpretation, the stage was set for the arrival of the new order.

Ellie didn't have time to run anymore. She focused on the great flood and was seeking higher ground. She didn't get to see the great Rose Rock crystal rising, but she saw the arrival of the new eastern star order; Christ was about to appear. The new order was generated by the earth tipping on its axis, the rising of the seven temples, each pushing a rose quartz crystal to open like flower petals. New Jerusalem was about to arrive. In deep thought, high atop the grey granite cliff rocks, Ellie leaned against the mossy glyphs. As Ellie waited for the water to recede, the arrival of the twin Thunderbirds, she sketched a map of all her travels (Figure 12). The duality of twins, she mused.

When the orange and red sky birds appeared, her mood abruptly changed. Ellie shook in her boots, after all what had she done for Christ in her self-preoccupied freedom quest. The experience had greatly humbled her, allowing her to change her quest to serve Him first. Ellie was stunned that she had a second chance, just a moment, to change her ways, because so few do and remain in the realm of their own selfishness. Ellie now realized that she was a helper, a link in the cosmic chain. She was a tiny part as the silver key of knowledge had unlocked a series of events that had brought about the timely changes.

However, perhaps the Temple rising had nothing to do with Christ's return, perhaps it was just the home of a sleeping dragon. Either way, it was a compelling event that was not destined for immediate interpretation.

ILLUSTRATIONS

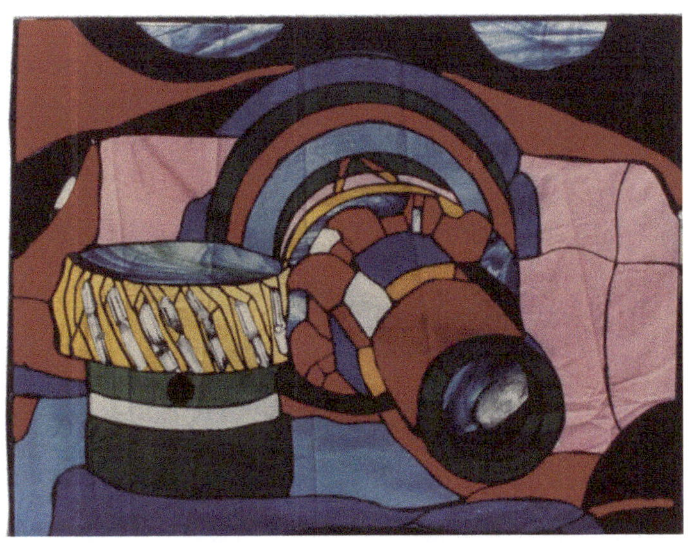

Figure 1. Sportster Cam Shaft Drive Gear

Figure 2. Spirit Rock Window

Figure 3. Sacred Lake Scythe Dragon Battle

Figure 4. Sacred Lake Dragonfly Window

Figure 5. Stony Lake Temple Window

Figure 5B: Stony Lake Temple

Figure 6. Stony Lake Temple Rising Window

Figure 6B: Stony Lake Temple Rising Window

Figure 7. Boathouse Glyph Map Window

Figure 8. Distant Spider Mountain Towers

Figure 9. Big Cave Elder Room

Figure 10. Big Cave Treasure Room

Figure 11. Rose Crystal Rising

Figure 12. Road Queen Journey Map

ABOUT THE AUTHOR

J. Price is an avid author, artist, motorcycle mechanic and researcher who lives and rides in the U.S.A.

www.ingramcontent.com/pod-product-compliance
Lightning Source LLC
Chambersburg PA
CBHW061127100726
47911CB00013B/707